Why Did My Brain Make Me Say It?

'I love the variety of subject matter in Sarah's book and the many different ways she finds to approach writing her poems. Humorous, thoughtful and surprising at times. She is a poet whose work deserves to be widely read.' — **BRIAN MOSES**

'In this collection you will find people, creatures, fun, sadness, stillness, noise, puzzles and brain-tickling cleverness. You will discover a confident playfulness, keen observation, delightful twists and impactful last lines. There's not a letter out of place.'
— **CORAL RUMBLE**

Published by TROIKA
First published 2024

Troika Books Ltd, Well House, Green Lane, Ardleigh CO7 7PD, UK
www.troikabooks.com

Text copyright © Sarah Ziman 2024
Collection designed and typeset by White Stone Pages

A CIP catalogue record for this book is available from the British Library

ISBN 978-1-912745-39-5
1 3 5 7 9 10 8 6 4 2

Printed in Poland at Totem.com.pl

why did my brain make me say it?

troika

To Jake and Zac, with all my love
(You just lost The Game)

Contents

Introduction

When I was asked to write an introduction to *Why Did My Brain Make Me Say It?*, I worried about what I was going to say. What *is* this collection all about? What *was* my brain thinking when I wrote these poems? What if my brain made me say something stupid in the introduction which I would regret once it was in print?

But that's the interesting thing about brains, as well as the wonder of poetry – they can both do the unexpected. While the title of this collection comes from a line in my poem *'Faux Pas'* – where the speaker is bemoaning an embarrassing slip of the tongue at school – it can also be a question to ask ourselves when we write.

Why does *my* brain come up with one way to describe something, and my friend's brain with something else entirely? We could both be looking at the same thing, or experiencing the same event, or given the same prompt – and we'd still create completely different interpretations of it. Why does a particular idea – perhaps a hairdresser being faced with Medusa's alarmingly lively locks, or a packed lunch getting progressively stranger as the week goes on – suddenly pop into your head, seemingly from nowhere? I'm still trying to find out, but putting them into a poem seems like the best way to deal with the chatter.

Oh yes, one thing I do know about my brain is that it can be very noisy – probably to make up for the fact that it's also very dark in there. This is due to my aphantasia, which means I can't create images when I think. I didn't realise until I was an adult that most other people could 'picture' their thoughts in their heads – I suppose I thought this and 'mind's eye' were just figures of speech, because they made you think of something you could see in real life!

Brains are funny old things though – everyone's is different. Mine has this talkative inner voice instead of a mind's eye, but apparently that's another thing that not everyone has. I think not being able to form pictures in my head might explain why I particularly enjoy playing with how to present poems on the page, or how they sound when read aloud. It might also mean I'm a bit more tuned into the spoken word to compensate – this could be why so many of my poems are in first person, or have a lot of dialogue.

However your brain works, I hope you enjoy some of the ideas that came from mine.

Best wishes,

Sarah Ziman

Hi-ku

Howdy! Hey! Salaam!
Top o' the morning! Hello!
Wotcher! Whassup? Yo!

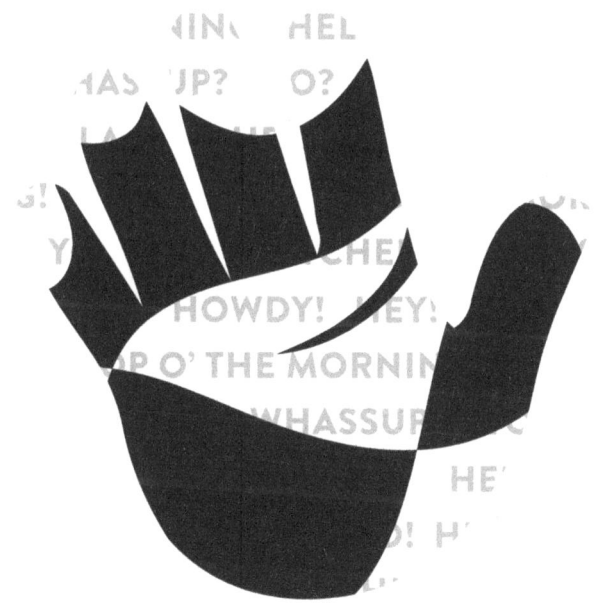

Packed Lunch

On Monday,
I opened my lunchbox and I had:
A ham sandwich,
Some cheese and onion crisps,
And an apple.

On Tuesday,
I opened my lunchbox and I had:
A cheese sandwich,
Some ham and onion crisps,
And an apple.

On Wednesday,
I opened my lunchbox and I had:
A ham and cheese sandwich,
Some apple crisps,
And an onion.

On Thursday,
I opened my lunchbox and I had:
A sandy ham,
Some crispy onion,
And a cheesy witch.

On Friday,
I had school dinners.

Opposites

My hair's curly / Hers is straight
I wake early / She sleeps late

I'm a dog fan / She likes cats
I wear hoodies / She wears hats

I do ballet / She does judo
I say Scrabble / She says Ludo

I like maths / She likes art
I win races / She won't start

I've got brown skin / She's got pink
I sing solo / She'll lip-sync

I want sunshine / She wants snow
If I say yes / Then she says no

I crunch crisps / She bakes cake
I'm a veggie / She eats steak

I've got brothers / She's an only
I like peace / She gets lonely

My hair's curly / Hers is straight
She's my friend / I'm her mate

New Girl/Merch Newydd

When I started at the Welsh school,
I was so shy.
I didn't understand much.
Just how to say my name really:
> *Chloe dw i*
and *un* (1), *dau* (2), *tri* (3).
I thought I almost understood
how Ahsan must have felt,
when he started at my old school,
a refugee.

After a week at *yr ysgol Gymraeg*,
I still felt *swil*,
but I understood a little bit more.
I could say 'Good morning' to our teacher:
> *Bore da, Mrs Morgan!*
I could say whether I wanted *afal* or *oren*,
when the fruit came out at snack time.
And when they served up fish and chips for *cinio*,
I definitely didn't want any yucky green *pys* –
> *Ych a fi!*

Now **yn yr ysgol Gymraeg**,
I understand **tipyn bach** more again.
The words are letting me catch up,
not all skipping away together,
too fast for me to follow.
I've got **ffrindiau** in the playground too:
    Eleri, Seren a Sophie
and an invitation to **parti Seren**, this weekend.
I'll wrap her gift in **papur** with silver stars,
just like her name.

Glossary

Chloe dw i - I am Chloe
un (een) - one
dau (die) - two
tri (tree) - three
yr ysgol Gymraeg (uhr us-gol gum-rye-gh) - the Welsh School
Swil - shy
Bore da (Bo reh da) - Good morning
afal - apple
oren - orange
cinio (kin-yoh) - lunch/dinner
pys - peas
Ych a fi - YUK!
tipyn bach (tipin bach - like the composer) - a little bit
ffrindiau (frin-dee-eye) - friends
parti - party
Seren - a girl's name, also meaning star

Reasons my little sister cried this week

- Biscuit broke – could not be mended
- Asked to brush her teeth – offended
- Wanted blue cup, not the pink
- Given blue cup – kicked up stink
- Refused to walk – lay down on path
- Stopped from drinking bubble bath
- Not allowed to pull cat's tail
- Not allowed to lick a snail
- Not allowed to throw Mum's phone
- Granny told her that she'd grown
- Unable to push down tree
- From a distance – saw a bee
- Dropped her ice cream – BIG disaster
- Cross that I can run much faster
- Left at pre-school – howled in vain
- Picked up later – same again
- Did not want help to do up shoes
- Found banana had a bruise
- Dolly's socks would not go on
- Duck ate bread she'd meant for swan
- Jigsaw puzzle proved quite tricky
- Toast and honey was 'too sticky'
- Kicked her ball at goal and missed
- Not happy that I wrote this list!

Poet who doesn't know it

Today in literacy,
we learned about synonyms.
It was quite interesting, enthralling and absorbing,
not to mention captivating.
I used some of them in my acrostic poem, verse and ode,
which was:

Arresting
Compelling
Riveting
Original
Striking
Thought-provoking
Impressive, and
Curious.

Our teacher, instructor, professor and pedagogue,
told us that next lesson we'd be learning
about simile, onomatopoeia, and alliteration.
And we were like, **WHOA, WOW, NO WAY!**
He laughed and said we'd got the idea,
but how about we write a haiku for homework?

I was going to
but I couldn't remember
the syllable count.

Love/Hate

You're the cherry on my sundae
The ketchup on my chips
The jelly in my trifle
The giftshop on my trips
The olives on my pizza
The PJs for my cat
The cheese on my spaghetti
The bobble on my hat
The bubbles in my bath tub
The blackbird in my pie
The fourth leaf on my clover
The apple of my eye.

You're the spider in my bathtub
The stone that's in my shoe
The maggot in my apple
The mushroom in my stew
The homework at the weekend
The dog poo at the park
The plastic in my ocean
The LEGO in the dark
The filling at the dentist
The hiccups that won't stop
The long queue for the toilet
The weasel in my pop.

Faux Pas

I'm running away to the circus,
I'm joining another school –
where's my backpack?
I'm seeking my fortune –
      I've broken the cardinal rule.

WHY did my brain make me say it?
I'm sitting here baffled and numb –
they all heard me,
I just can't believe it –
      I called Miss McAllister *'Mum'*!

Crime and Punishment

I picture it in a pickle jar;
It fills me up with dread.
I've heard that if you're *really* bad,
You're sent to see...the **HEAD**.

Extra

He's extra cheeky
extra fun –
No smile?
He's got an extra one.

He's extra friendly
extra kind –
He's extra-specially
designed.

Though some things he
finds extra tough –
He's extra good
at trying stuff.

With extra help
he can succeed –
He's extra stubborn,
that's agreed.

He's extra brave
much more than me –
He really is
extraordinary.

There's extra joy
in Charlie's home –
and just
one
extra chromosome.

(**Note:** *Having an extra chromosome at
birth causes a genetic condition called
Down's syndrome, which can result in
health issues and learning difficulties.
Children with Down's syndrome have
grown up to be successful actors, TV
presenters, models, entrepreneurs
and more!*)

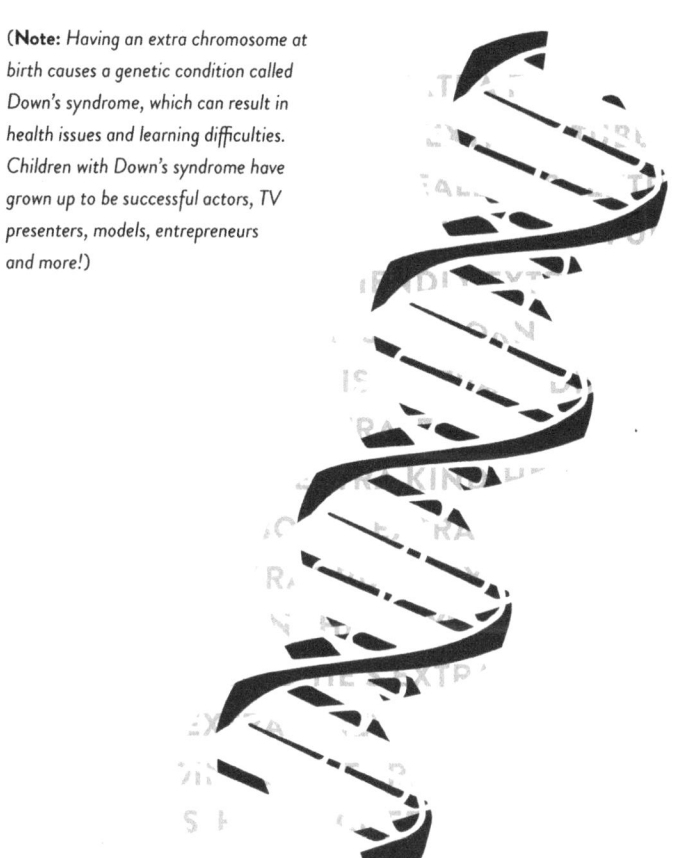

Secret Weapon

I always have some Blu Tack
in my pocket.
When I get distracted,
it helps to squash it.
Mum got cross
when I forgot it
and it went through the wash.
But she doesn't realise,
that it's my secret weapon.

Just a little piece on the nose
and a normal paper aeroplane
is a stunt plane!
Has your tooth come out –
just before school photos?
A tiny bit – and ta-dah!
(Miss says that wasn't my finest hour.)

She wasn't very happy
when I was flicking it at Freddy either,
that time it was alien bogies.
But when I fixed her wobbly chair
at Parents' Evening –
she was quite impressed.

It's my secret weapon for Sports Day too,
but don't tell anyone –
I've been the undisputed egg-and-spoon champ
ever since Year 3.

Once, I made it into two rings,
and me and Ella-Mae wore them all through lunch.
But afterwards she turned hers into a dolphin,
so I turned mine into a troll.
Miss says that if I ever finish this poem,
perhaps we can use some to put it on the wall.

One-upper

My aunt had a baby –
>> *her* auntie had two,

I caught a cold –
>> but *she* had the flu.

My mum can sing –
>> but *hers* is a popstar,

When I got a scooter –
>> *they* got a car.

We got a new car –
>> *her* dad bought a plane,

We're going to Butlins –
>> *she's* going to Spain.

We're going to Spain –
>> *she's* off to the moon,

If my name was May –
>> then *hers* would be June.

She's *such* a one-upper

She's always on top

If you bought a T-shirt
>> Then *she'd* own the shop.

Her house is the **BIGGEST**
Her grandma the *oldest*
Her pet is the *cutest*
Her ice-cream the *coldest*
Her hair is the *longest*
Her shoes cost the *most* –

There's no doubt about it:
      she's best at the BOAST!

Pre-emptive Strike

Had a biscuit.
Sister nicked it.
What she doesn't know –
I licked it.

Psst! Pass it on!

If you share some sweets,
you've done a good thing.
You feel good, but —
you don't have the sweets anymore.
And what if there are five of you,
but you only have four sweets?
Someone gets left out.
But you can share a poem
with as many people as you like,
and it will never run out.
People who like it can share it too,
with anyone THEY like.
Their nan, their step-dad,
their baby brother,
the lady who works in the fish-and-chip shop—
Anybody!

Like a smile a poem can be passed on.

Maybe YOU heard it from someone older,
who first heard it when they were your age.
They might have heard it in the playground:

chanted,

      skipped

           or clapped

                 to it,

and remembered it all of their life.
Every time they hear it,
it takes them back to their childhood.
Poems can be magic like that.
Perhaps, now you know it,
one day, YOU'LL be the grandparent who passes it on.
Maybe it will be *this* poem—
the one you're reading right now!
Like love,
a poem is something
that gets **bigger** the more it's shared.

Christmas Confusion

When I was but a tiny child,
The vicar came to call:

'Do you sing *Away in a Manger*?'

I said, 'No, we sing in the hall'.

Winter Solstice

By a cockerel's step*
By the snow's settling hush
By the gap between notes
in the song of the thrush

By the slow-spreading crack
in the acorn beneath
By the whisk of the brush
of the fox on the heath

By the tiniest increments
light makes its way,
surely and steadily
back to the
day.

*a cockerel's step is a small measurement, and the term for the winter solstice in Welsh
(**cam ceiliog**)

Spring!

Freshly painted pheasants in every field,
newly emerged from their chrysalises.
The just-fledged lambs
take their first wobbling flights,
and the ponds are filled with the croaking
of spawning daffodils.

Spring!

Squirrels begin to lay their beautiful speckled eggs
as the chaffinches burst into bloom,
brightening the forest floor once again.
Listen carefully and you may hear
the drumming of the ducklings against the dead wood
high in the canopy above.

Spring!

Fieldmice flit from flower to flower,
and the otter swarm follow their queen
to new nesting grounds.
Ah! What it is to be alive!
When the wild garlic hatches,
and the voice of the mole is heard in our land.

YOU ARE A READER!

Once upon a time the ancients carved their tales in stone
Nowadays there's kindle or an app upon your phone
Book yourself some book time, but be sure to make it known –
That...**YOU...ARE...A READER!**

Whether you like comics, or non-fiction, or a laugh
Whether you're in bed, at school, or sitting in the bath
Whether it's got pictures or the author's autograph –
YOU...ARE...A READER!

Maybe you wear glasses, or a special font is best
Books in Braille are brilliant – the pages are IMPRESSED!
Audio is awesome – is it reading? Take a guess –
YES! **YOU... ARE...A READER!**

Whether you like fantasy or mysteries or crime
Whether you like magazines or poetry and rhyme
Whether you read speedily or like to take your time
YOU...ARE...A READER!

Read the lyrics video to every YouTube song
Read a tiny haiku or a series that is loooooooong
Now you've read this poem, so you really can't go wrong –
Look...**YOU...ARE...A READER!**

Lie-ku

I really don't mind
That I wasn't invited –
I'm busy that day

I don't want to play
I prefer to sit and watch
I'm too tired for tag

I'm not feeling sick
My tummy isn't churning
Something's in my eye

Everything is fine
There's nothing I need to say
There's no need to ask

Growing a Poem

A poem begins as a seed
buried deep inside the imagination.
It may land in your mind
with a touch as gentle as thistledown,
or with the sudden shock
of a conker, splitting its spiked fortress
like a cannonball.
You will know when it arrives.

Add the warmth of a memory,
or today's sunbeams.
You will want to keep it well watered.
Tears of laughter perhaps,
or the salty tang of sadness.
Either will work here to germinate your idea.
Listen.
Can you hear your poem slowly waking?

If you're lucky, your poem may shoot up
like Jack's beanstalk.
Vigorous and sure of itself –
an immediate adventure.
Follow it at once.
There's certain to be a reward
if you ascend far enough into the clouds.
Trust your poem will hold you.

Why Did My Brain Make Me Say It?

Your poem could be thorny at first –
as impenetrable as the briars
around Sleeping Beauty's castle.
That's alright.
You have time, and the tools you need.
Train and prune your words carefully,
snipping out the dead wood.
Your poem will bloom eventually.

Delight, as your poem takes root,
in somebody else's heart.

Eating Out

I'd like the burger please.
No, not the macaroni cheese.
Yes, I'm sure it's very nice.
Yes, I do like it at home.
I just don't fancy it today.
I'd like the burger.

Fish fingers are good too, I agree.
I know that's what they mean.
I'm not put off by them calling them goujons.
Honestly.
I know that I wouldn't have to eat the tartare sauce.
It's just that I'd like the burger.

I don't think I eat too much red meat.
You were suggesting sausage and mash a minute ago.
That's red meat, isn't it?
I don't ALWAYS get the same thing.
I might have had the burger last time,
but that was months ago.
It's not my fault that we're here again the day I JUST
HAPPEN to fancy a burger.

Yes, I saw that they do a jacket potato.
With baked beans.
Or tuna.
And a side salad.
Very good, I'm sure.
Well then, you HAVE the wild boar ragù with tagliatelle.
I'm not stopping you.
But I'm your father, and I'd like the burger.

Consequences

Cheesecake,
Trifle, Treacle Tart,
Baked Alaska —
that's to start.
Apple Pie, Rice Pud, Banoffee,
Crème Brûlée And Sticky Toffee,
Rhubarb Crumble, Spotted Dick,
Chocolate Brownie?
Bring it quick!
Eton Mess, Jam Roly-Poly,
Giant Knickerbocker Glory,
Profiteroles, Banana Split;
Just some Pavlova,
then I'll quit—

Ugh, but how my
stomach hurts—
I guess they call
that... just
DESSERTS!

Pet Peeve

They're not the most exciting pet.
You can spend ages peering through the glass,
but they don't really do much,
and of course, you can't stroke them.
There's a lot more interaction with a cat.
Up and down, up and down they go,
completely directionless.
You might even say gormless,
the way their mouths open and shut all the time.
Then sometimes they stop moving altogether,
and just sit there, gazing straight ahead.
It's only when food appears,
that they look lively again.
They are pretty though, with their different colours,
I'll give them that.
I've heard they only have a five-second memory.
Wouldn't surprise me at all,
I've not been able to teach them ANY tricks.

Still, at least humans are low maintenance.

Copycat, by ~~Ella Mae~~ Kate

She's copied my T-shirt
She's copied my shoes
She's with me at lunchtime
to see what I choose.
She draws the same pictures!
She reads the same books!
We've got the same coats,
on identical hooks!
Mum baked me a birthday cake
shaped like a horse,
I went to her party –
she copied, of course!
A cake with a pony,
I KNEW it! I'd guessed!
(She'd copy my GLASSES
but passed the eye test.)
I got a new goldfish –
then she got one too,
I christened mine Jaws,
so hers is Jaws 2.
Our Christmas Nativity –
THAT was a sight –
apparently TWO stars
were shining that night!
It's just SO annoying
I'm really perplexed
I can't help but wonder

what she'll copy next:
My bobbles? My school bag?
My favourite song?
My hairstyle? My notebook?
Good guesses – but wrong!
It's made me SO ANGRY
the WORST thing of all –
MY poem's got HER name on,
up on the wall!

Anticipation

Today my friend is coming round for tea;
I'll have that fizzy feeling all day long,
which ties a shining string from her to me.
Today my friend is coming round for tea.
It's like a gift that no one else can see;
my feet have got a smile, my heart a song.
Today my friend is coming round for tea –
I'll have that fizzy feeling all day long.

Medusa goes to the Hairdresser

Sit down madam, cup of tea?
Let's get this off... OH!
Gracious me.

Cobras... Vipers... Mambas too?
You know, I *think* we'll skip shampoo.

I see now why you wore the hat –
Perhaps an up-do – nice French plait?

Or maybe ribbons – tied in bunches?
Just checking –
have they had their lunches?

Oh dear, and now my comb is missing –
Won't...stop...writhing...PLEASE...STOP HISSING!

At last.

I've tamed them.

Verrrry chic!

I'll fetch the mirror – take a peek!

You must! You're like a film star clone –

Madam?

My gosh...!

She's turned to STONE!

Riddle

A king, with made-to-measure throne
My face as blank and smooth as stone
A silver shovel breaks my crown,
And soldiers take my gold to town.

WHAT AM I?

Tadcu's Lemons

In the morning,
Mamgu always made his tea
in the lemons cup.
'I'll be needing two sugars in that one!'
he used to say.
Now, I don't know whether it's poured away
or if she drinks them both,
but by lunchtime
it still sits on the draining board
next to hers, with the oranges.

Tadcu is pronounced Tad-key (Grandad)
Mamgu is pronounced Mam-ghee (Granny)

Lemonau Tadcu

Yn y bore,
roedd Mamgu bob amser yn gwneud ei disgled
yn y cwpan lemonau.
'Dw i eisiau dau siwgr yn yr un yna!'
roedd e'n arfer dweud.
Nawr, wn i ddim a yw wedi'i arllwys
neu a yw hi'n yfed y ddau,
ond erbyn amser cinio
mae'n dal i eistedd ar y bwrdd draenio
wrth ymyl ei chwpan, gyda'r orennau.

Translation: Ness Owen

How to live forever

Sometimes time goes S...O...O...O
S...L...O...O...O...W...L...Y.
It's as if everything has stopped and you'll never get any older.
If you could save all those bits up,
you could live forever!
Like —
the night before Christmas when you just want it to be morning,
but you don't know if it's dark because it's the middle of the night,
or if it's that kind of dark where you're allowed to get up,
just this once.
Or the week leading up to your birthday,
which almost definitely contains twice as many sleeps as usual.
Or when it's ONE HUNDRED YEARS till lunchtime and
you're seriously wasting away,
and you're not allowed a snack.
But worst of ALL —
is when your mum meets someone she knows
at the supermarket, or on the way home
and they get to having a bit of a chat
in the middle of the vegetable aisle
or just outside the post office
and all you can do
is scuff your feet
and huff and sigh
and feel time
turning
into

t

r

e

a

c

l

e

Seriously, at this rate you could be a million years old!

But then — FOILED!

Mum lets you have an hour on the Xbox when you get home —
AndtimemysteriouslyspeedsupagainlikeUsainBolt.

Things Siân's house has that our house doesn't

- A doorbell that plays a tune
- Stairs with gaps in them ~~which I'm NOT scared of~~
- A tortoise who lives in the back garden
- Pizza Fridays!
- A funny smell that no one else notices
- A creaking sound I only hear at night
- That photo of me with no teeth, framed on the mantlepiece
- My dad

Granny and Grandad

Make-believer
Ouch-reliever
Jam-maker
Cake-baker
Book-reader
Garden-weeder
Veg-grower
Hug-bestower
Bird-spotter
List-jotter
Coffee-drinker
Sunshine-thinker
World-explorer

Cap-wearer
Poem-sharer
Shopping-fetcher
Sofa-stretcher
Campfire-lighter
Story-writer
Quiz-winner
Wide-grinner
Kite-flyer
Paper-buyer
Glasses-loser
Armchair-snoozer
Loud-snorer

Me-adorer!

Riddle

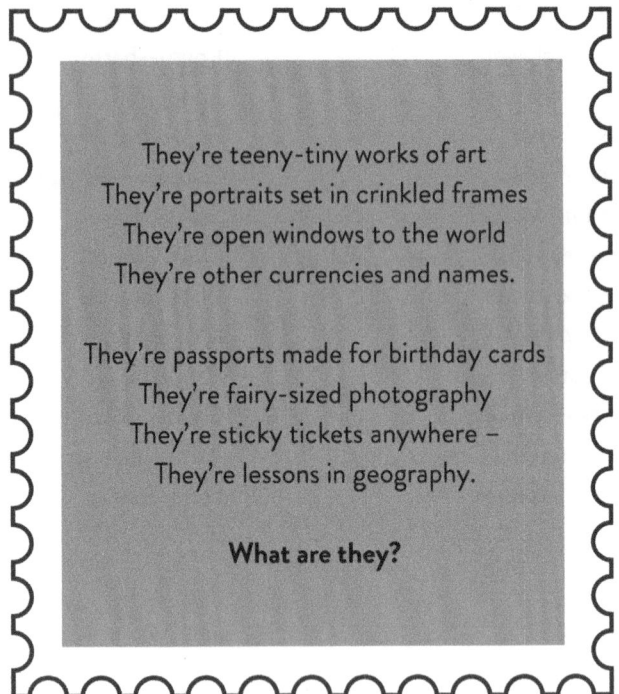

They're teeny-tiny works of art
They're portraits set in crinkled frames
They're open windows to the world
They're other currencies and names.

They're passports made for birthday cards
They're fairy-sized photography
They're sticky tickets anywhere –
They're lessons in geography.

What are they?

Answer: STAMPS

Timetable

Oh no! I dropped this timetable poem and all the subjects got mixed up. Can you put them back in the right place? There's a clue in every line.

Please lend me your *notes* from ....

(My mum wrote a note for ....)

I'm *praying* there's no .... homework

J'ai oublié que c'est aujourd'hui. (........................)

.... test! I need the *solutions*

Please **take** these .... lessons **away**!

.... again? Well, that's *novel*

Yay, ... — shall I have chips today?

More *chips* to *byte* in ....

Then .... just goes on for YEARS

Thank goodness — the final bell's ringing,

And .... is greeted with cheers!

FRENCH	**MUSIC**
LUNCH	**R.E.**
HISTORY	**ENGLISH**
MATHS	**SCIENCE**
COMPUTERS	**P.E**
HOME TIME	

Dear Mrs Kent

I fear I must write home to say
the way that Clark behaved today,
fell rather short in most respects
of standards that this school expects.

It pains me to call Clark a cheat,
but when he reads my answer sheet
with X-ray vision, I'm perplexed –
are we *quite* sure he needs those specs?

And levitating in the hall?
It's not acceptable. AT ALL.
I quote: *'You told us not to RUN –*
and flying really is more fun'.

But using 'freeze breath' on my tea?
Well, THAT was the last straw for me.
It turned to ice, and cracked my cup
and frankly now – I'm quite fed up.

Don't get me wrong. His future's bright,
if he could just learn wrong from right.
Might I suggest a sticker chart?

Yours sincerely,

Mrs Hart

<u>P.S.</u>
A note on uniform:
Now that the days are getting warm,
the shorts are fine – but could he stop
the wearing underpants on top?

Felicity

Felicity had always lived next door;
we used to see each other every day.
But she's not here to play with anymore,
since they packed the van and drove their things away.

We used to see each other every day
in the playground. Now I don't know what to do.
Since they packed the van and drove their things away,
a little piece of me went with them too.

In the playground now, I don't know what to do;
I can't help thinking that I'll see her face.
A little piece of me went with them too,
and years of friendship gone without a trace.

I can't help thinking that I'll see her face,
but she's not here to play with anymore.
And years of friendship gone without a trace —
Felicity had *always* lived next door.

Space

There's a space on the kitchen floor,
where she used to sit.
We'd got so used to just stepping around,
that once she wasn't there –
we'd somehow trip over thin air.

There's a space in the back of our car,
where she used to ride.
No mud – no ancient tennis balls, all chewed.
No favourite sticks she chose –
the windows clean, without her nose.

There's a space in our family,
where she used to be.
Her name was the very first word I said.
She was a true best friend –
from my beginning, till her end.

There's a space in our hearts,
where she'll always fit.
'You've got some big pawprints to fill', says Dad
as I pat our new pup –
but somehow, new space opens up.

Sleep Pattern

I have to go to bed
Please don't insist that
It's far too early
My eyes aren't heavy
The sky's not even dark
I'm yawning
It's ridiculous to tell me
Read just one more chapter
Sing another song
Run about outside
Finish watching TV
It's never been more important to
Look at what time it is
After all
Why am I in my pyjamas?

(Now read from bottom to top)

Summer

Summer's a picnic rug, six weeks spread wide,
Summer's the bell, you'll be running outside.
Summer's the summit, you'll freewheel downhill.
Summer's the soft drink they let you refill.

Summer's a butterfly, spreading its wings,
Summer's a kite, with lengthening strings.
Summer's a sweet you'll dissolve on your tongue.
Summer's the season you'll always be young.

Summer's a swing to go high as you dare,
Summer's escape and the wind in your hair.
Summer's your city, your village, your town,
Summer's your poem; so *go* – write it down.

Performance Piece

(An artwork consisting of a banana duct-taped to a wall was recently eaten by a hungry gallery visitor in South Korea, who then stuck the empty skin back up. The piece – called 'Comedian' – originally sold for £91,000. Can you guess which of the items below have been displayed as art?)

The peel from your satsuma –
Is it ART?
An empty tin of tuna –
Is it ART?
A gigantic stack of socks,
piled up in a cardboard box –
Is it ART?
Is it ART?
Is it ART?

A dishevelled unmade bed –
Is it ART?
All the stuff that's in the shed –
Is it ART?
A bare room with neon lights,
filled with seven tons of rice –
Is it ART?
Is it ART?
Is it ART?

Screwed-up paper from the bin –
Is it ART?
Getting toothpaste on your chin –
Is it ART?
An old sandwich growing mould,
Or a toilet made of gold –
Is it ART?
Is it ART?
Is it ART?

If it hasn't got a frame –
Is it ART?
If it's purely done for fame –
Is it ART?
Is a sculpture more exciting,
than the poem we're reciting –?
Is it ART?
Is it ART?
IS IT ART?

Rumours

They're crossing our class
from the front to the back —
I heard it from Amit
He heard it from Jack.
He heard it from Martha
who then told Shanice,
who told it to Patience
(best friends with Patrice).
Patrice then told Hannah
who said to Adele:

'The stork's paid a visit to Mrs Patel!'

I wondered to Eddie:
'A stork has been seen?
Is that like a heron?
But what does it mean?'
Eddie just shrugged
and whispered to Jake,
who then told the lunch queue:
'It's not a mistake!
You can ask ANYONE,
that's what I heard —

Poor Mrs P was attacked by a bird!'

Why Did My Brain Make Me Say It?

What bird? An eagle?
Could it be her pet?
I heard a crocodile!
I saw the vet!
She fought off a tiger!
I heard she BOUGHT three!
I *know the story —*
No, listen to **ME***!*
Everyone shouting
a hullabaloo —

'Mrs Patel left to open a zoo!'

A laugh from our teacher
(Her name is Miss Trent —
and she came to teach us
when Mrs P went)
'Good heavens children —
what IS it you've heard?
Fighting with tigers?
Attacked by a bird?!
There's no need for worry
No cause for alarm
Her BABY arrived —
She's come to no harm!

Troika Firsts

A lovely sweet baby,
no claws and no beak —
delivered quite safely
the end of last week.
Let's clear up these rumours
and make lovely cards,
to send our good wishes
and fondest regards.'
'*Delivered!*' mused Martha,
 '*And here in no time?*

The baby was ordered from Amazon Prime!'

Her name is Alexa!
My aunt saw the van!
Well, **MY** *uncle knows the delivery man...*

Which bee to be?

Buzzy, fuzzy?
Bumblebee.

Kind of clumsy?
Stumblebee.

Acrobatic?
Tumblebee.

Undramatic?
Humblebee.

What's that? Speak up!
Mumblebee.

Grumpy streak? Yup –
Grumblebee.

Faintly flustered?
Fumblebee.

Nice with custard?
Crumblebee!

Recipe for a Wasp

Take a gallon of petrol
from the BMW
that overtook your dad on the motorway
that time he said a rude word,
Your baby brother's tantrum
the morning your mum went back to work,
An argument with your best friend
and your sister's smirk.
Boil violently.
Sieve the mixture through the jumper your gran made.
The itchy one with yellow and black stripes
and a head-hole that's too tight.
Stir in some English mustard with a freshly sharpened pencil.
This *must* be HB.

Next you will need:
The tick of the clock outside the head teacher's office
Some nails bitten to the quick
The smell of hospitals
LEGO trodden on in bare feet
and a Sunday evening sense of doom.
Beat with a splintery wooden spoon.
Pour into your mould
and bake at ten thousand degrees Fahrenheit
in the centre of the sun.
Allow to cool a little, and admire your insect.
A heat-seeking missile
in a bombshell body.

Release at a picnic...

and RUN.

Cinnabar Caterpillars

On the waste ground, in dusty midsummer,
prospect for gold and you'll find the ragwort's bloom.
Look closer – see how it's decked with bright scarves?
Hufflepuff house, or Watford football fans
cheering the season on.
Tipped into a curious palm
they ammonite immediately,
coiling tight till danger's passed.
Back on their patch, they can strip the plant bare –
leaf, stalk and petal –
in a matter of days.
      Tiny tigers, devouring the sun.

In-betweener

Well, here is a puzzle I can't seem to fix –
Am I in Year 7? Or still a Year 6?
Primary's over – it's finished, all done.
There's no doubt about it; the summer's begun.
I've taken my books home,
I've emptied my tray.
No need to rehearse
for the end-of-school play.
The hooks are all empty.
My polo shirt's signed.
I've sat all my SATs,
Left my first school behind.
So, secondary's coming – a total clean slate –
but that's in September, all summer to wait.
I need a new backpack,
I'll wear a new tie.
The teachers don't know me
and...neither do I.
Just who will I *be* –
when I enter this school?
A miniscule fish,
in a gigantic pool.
Yes, I am a puzzle I can't seem to fix –
Not quite in Year 7, no longer Year 6.

New School Shoes

Box fresh but they're total nasties
Kind of look like Cornish pasties
Why can't Mum see these are ghastly –
NEW SCHOOL SHOES?

Know they'll turn my toes to mincemeat
Rather wear boots made of concrete
Like two cruise ships steering my feet –
NEW SCHOOL SHOES.

Made to walk around the shop floor
Clomping like an angry centaur
These kicks are a TOTAL eyesore –
NEW SCHOOL SHOES.

Street cred killed dead as the dodo
Shunned like poor old Quasimodo
Boring and safe as a Volvo –
NEW SCHOOL SHOES.

No way I'll be winning races
Tripping over too-long laces
Well OF COURSE I'm pulling faces –
NEW SCHOOL SHOES!

Leavers' Assembly

We're in our leavers' hoodies,
our names all on the back,
on stage one last assembly –
who will be first to crack?
Reception in the front row,
our parents at the rear,
Miss gives awards for 'kindness'
but we've yet to shed a tear.
We read out all our memories,
from Nursery to Year 6 –
we laugh at all the funny ones,
and 'aww' at old class pics.
They hand out all the yearbooks,
we filled with hopes and dreams –
and still we are all stoic,
at least – that's how it seems.
But then the music starts up,
and shoulder pressed to shoulder,
we sing a song of moving on,
goodbyes and getting older.
And suddenly the hall seems small,
this place we've known so long,
and we hug a little tighter
as we sing the leavers' song.
The mums and dads look wistful,
start dabbing at their eyes –
then our singing goes all croaky,
as half our choir cries.

The teachers hand out tissues,
though by then it's far too late –
the little ones are bawling
and the mums are in a state.
This starts off all the teachers
(we would not have had a *clue*)
But it seems they just might miss us –

We just might miss them too.

Return of the Swifts

Sky-scimitars sliced the day in two –
rowdy and fearless, controlling the air.

Unstoppable from Africa they flew,
assailing oceans, conquering continents –
as though fighter jets had roared through.

Boomeranging through the blue,
Screaming:

we're back!

we're back!

we're back!

Nature Walk

(**Note:** *skipper, comma, marbled white and peacock are all native UK butterflies*)

Blackbird

        magpie

red kite

        teasel

skipper

        comma,

rabbit?

        Weasel!

Watch out: nettles!

        – OW OW OW!

Dock leaf.

        Stile.

                Field with cow.

Skylarks

      poppies

badger's set...

COW PAT!

Puddle.

      Slightly wet.

Hand gel

      snack bar

marbled white

          peacock

buzzard's lazy flight.

Ragwort

      mallow

early bramble

      song thrush

oak tree

squirrel scramble.

Back through meadow

gate to pull...

dodge the cow pat...

COW IS BULL!

Blackbird

magpie

red kite

teasel

skipper

comma

rabbit

weasel!

Some days you sco **re** your fill of goals

And som**e** the pitch is full of holes

A heavy heart weighs **s**trong folks down,

But **l**ift your head, and bear your crown.

We can't be happy al**l** the time

Each summ**i**t takes a lengthy climb

If I could giv**e** you just one gift

Then it would be this mi**n**dset shift:

A falling ball **c**an still bounce back

And light shin**e**s through the smallest crack.

Rollercoaster

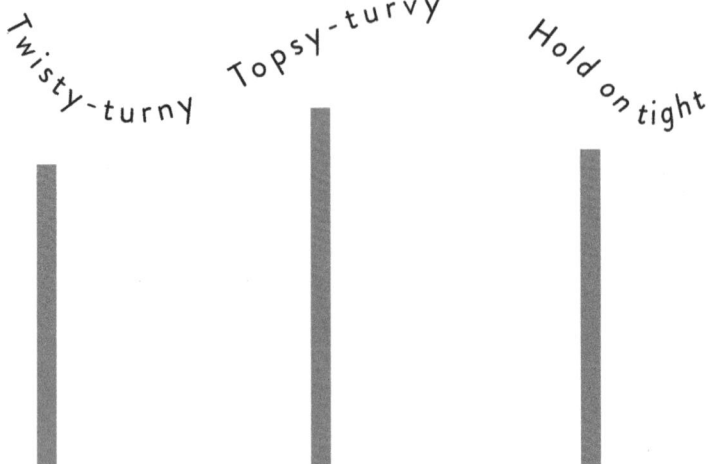

Twisty-turny

Topsy-turvy

Hold on tight

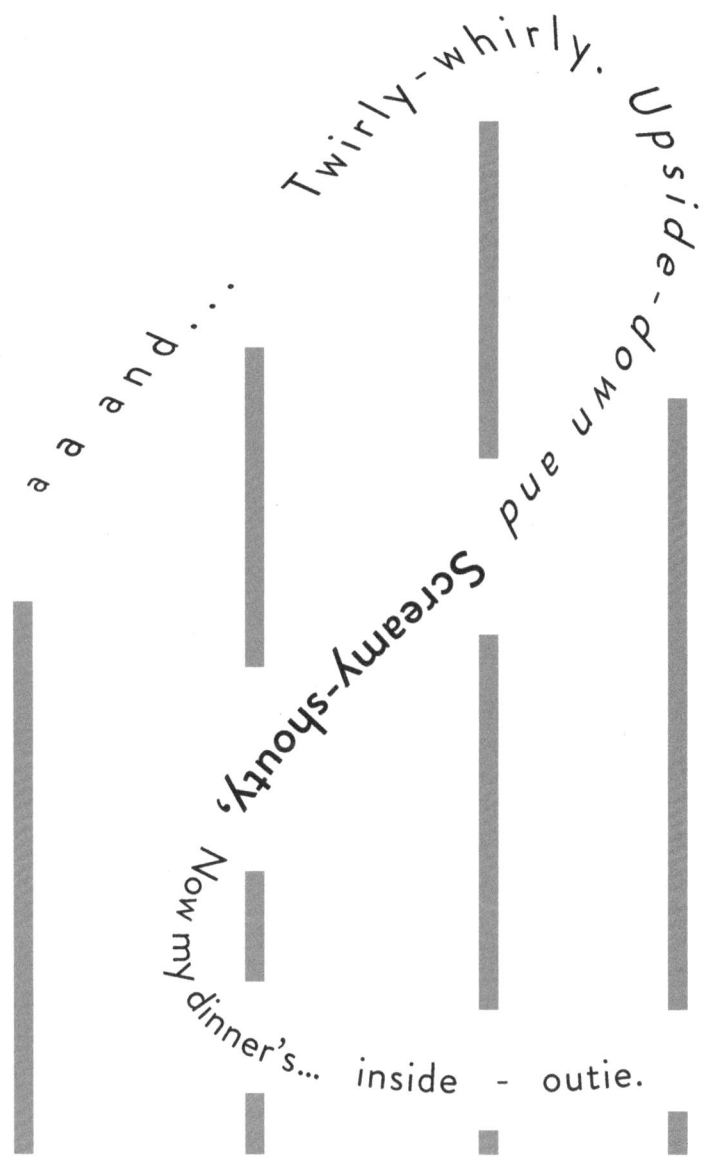

a a and... Twirly-whirly. Upside-down and Screamy-shouty, Now my dinner's... inside - outie.

Inventor

I love my onesie.
It's so soft and snuggly.
At the weekend
when I do most of my inventing,
I could lie around in it all day.

Aaaah, bliss.

The only problem is
it's a tiny bit tricky
if you need the loo.
I'm sure football mascots
have the same problem.
Or imagine being a pantomime horse.
Now that WOULD be awkward.

Anyway –

I thought up this great idea.
A two-piece onesie.
Called a twosie.
Cool huh?
Everyone would want one
and I'd make my fortune.

Genius.

Why Did My Brain Make Me Say It?

I had it all planned out.
A top half to pull down over your head
and a bottom half
to...well, you know,
pull up over your bottom.
But then my mum reminded me,
that a two-piece onesie
already exists,
and is called pyjamas.

Curses.
Back to the drawing board.

I'm working on a special pen
that doesn't have any ink,
so you can rub it out
if you make a mistake.

Bye-ku

Ta-ra! See ya! Ciao!
So long! Farewell, gotta fly!
Adios - Goodbye!

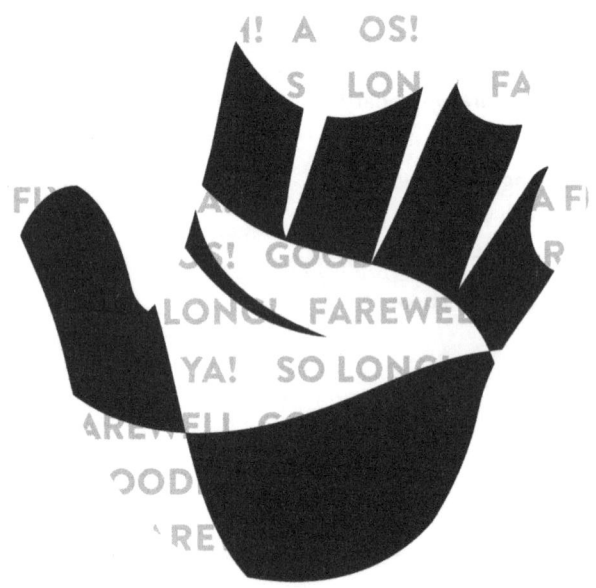

Acknowledgements

Thank you to my dad, who originally set me on the poetry path, to the Wednesday Advancers for their warm welcome and excellent advice, the Zig Zag crew for Monday critiques and NaPoWriMo madness, and of course the always supportive poetry people of Twitter/X for being generally brilliant in both in public and behind the scenes. If you've liked, commented, reposted or messaged about ANY of this poetry stuff – a massive thank you. You know who you are and I don't want to forget anyone!

Of course, a very BIG thank you to everyone at Troika involved in giving me this chance to share the contents of my brain in an actual book with my name on it – it's a dream come true! Also, thank you to Ness and to everyone who read an early copy and was kind enough to give me a quote – I am super grateful and owe you a pint (beer, wine, blood – whichever you need at the time).

Grateful thanks as well to every editor who has chosen to publish one of my poems in whatever format – lots of people who care very deeply about poetry for children are doing sterling work and I will continue to support small presses/ journals as much as I can, as well as submitting to traditional anthologies.

Finally, to my family – Ben who has stopped the house going to ruin around us as I write, and the boys for the inspiration and being my first readers.

About the Author

Sarah Ziman was born and grew up in the South Wales valleys, and is STILL learning Welsh. She wrote her first picture book at the age of six, having been heavily influenced by the 'Happy Families' series by Allan Ahlberg, and discovered poetry when her dad bought her a copy of *Please Mrs Butler* (also by Allan Ahlberg). She had a poem published in a book when she was 11, followed by one which travelled around as a poster on the London Underground when she was 13. She then had a little break of about 30 years, which she mostly spent lazing about eating crisps.

She won the YorkMix Poems for Children competition in 2021, has been highly commended for the Caterpillar Poetry Prize three times, and her poems can be found in magazines and anthologies worldwide. *Why Did My Brain Make Me Say It?* is her first solo collection for children.

You can find more about Sarah at www.sarahziman.co.uk

About this Collection

troika firsts

We love publishing poetry at Troika; it's been a pleasure and a privilege to work with the poets on our small list. The aim of Troika Firsts is to bring together a first full collection of poetry by a poet who may have had individual poems published in anthologies or elsewhere, but who has not yet published a cohesive collection of their work that showcases their individual and unique voice and style. We're delighted and thrilled to be publishing Sarah's first collection and to be launching this series which we hope will become part of our publishing programme annually.

The home of great children's books

Troika is a small independent children's
book publisher. We're based in the UK.

Follow us on social media

 @TroikaBooks

 @troikabooks

 @TroikaBooks